It's Just a Game

It's Just a Game

by John Farrell

Illustrated by John Emil Cymerman

Boyds Mills Press

Text copyright © 1999 by John Farrell
Illustrations copyright © 1999 by John Emil Cymerman
All rights reserved

Published by Caroline House
Boyds Mills Press, Inc.
A Highlights Company
815 Church Street
Honesdale, Pennsylvania 18431
Printed in China

Publisher Cataloging-in-Publication Data
Farrell, John.
   It's just a game / by John Farrell ; illustrated by John
Emil Cymerman.—1st ed.
   [32]p. : col. ill. ;   cm.
Summary: A soccer team learns that sports should be
played not only to win, but to have fun.
ISBN 1-56397-785-0
1. Sportsmanship-Fiction-Juvenile literature.
2. Soccer—Fiction—Juvenile literature.
[1. Sportsmanship—Fiction.
2. Soccer—Fiction.] I. Cymerman, John
Emil, ill. II. Title.
   [E]—dc21 1999 AC   CIP
Library of Congress Catalog Card
Number 99-60250

First edition, 1999

The text of this book is set in
17-point Bookman Medium.

10 9 8 7 6 5 4 3 2

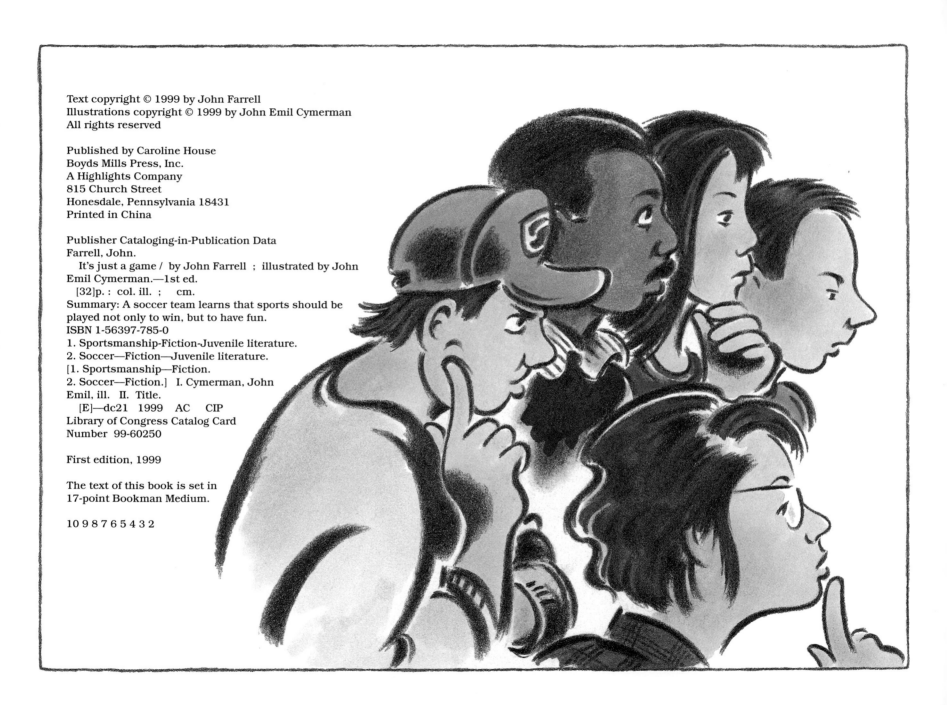

With love for the number one team in my heart—THE HOME TEAM—Ann Marie, Katie, Jack, Maggie, Colleen, and Patrick

—J. F.

To my father, Stefan Antoni Cymerman

—J. E. C.

The sun was shining bright
and the grass was oh so green.
We were laughing. We were singing.
It felt good to be a team.

We had new shorts and socks.
On our shirts they wrote
our names.

Then the other team appeared.
They came like soldiers to a war.
They were big and they were fast
and they looked mean.

Their coach was yelling at them.
He even called *us* names.

It's just a game! It's just a game!
We're only kids. We're not the pros.
We joined the team to learn and play
and have some fun.
We'll try our best to win,
but if we don't, there is no shame.
Please remember this:
"We're only kids. It's just a game!"

Then the game began.
We were nervous. We were scared.
They *were* big and they *were* fast,
but they *weren't* mean.

They did play well together.
They scored time and time again.

We made some good plays too.
We tried hard until the end.

And then the game was over.
We went and said, "Nice game."

Thoughts of ice cream quickly filled our brains.

Then we heard a grown-up shouting, "It's your fault! You're to blame!"

I wished someone would tell him,
"It's okay. It's just a game."

It's just a game! It's just a game!
We're only kids. We're not the pros.
We joined the team to learn and play
and have some fun.
We'll try our best to win,
but if we don't, there is no shame.
Please remember this:
"We're only kids. It's just a game!"

As our season went along,
we lost every game but one.

But we got better
and each practice
we learned something new.

Our coach says we're amazing!
Our team pictures came out great.
Our teamwork and
  our friendships grew and grew.

But when the last game ended,
another team had finished first.
They played well.
They played fair.
They were the best.

And though the medals went to them,
we feel like winners just the same.
We never quit and we know,
"It's just a game!"

It's just a game! It's just a game!
We're only kids. We're not the pros.
We joined the team to learn and play
and have some fun.
We'll try our best to win,
but if we don't, there is no shame.
Please remember this:
"We're only kids. It's just a game!"